James Johonnot

Book of Cats and Dogs, and Other Friends, for Little Folks

James Johonnot

Book of Cats and Dogs, and Other Friends, for Little Folks

ISBN/EAN: 9783744771795

Printed in Europe, USA, Canada, Australia, Japan

Cover: Foto ©Andreas Hilbeck / pixelio.de

More available books at **www.hansebooks.com**

BOOK OF
CATS AND DOGS,
AND
OTHER FRIENDS,
FOR LITTLE FOLKS.

By JAMES JOHONNOT.

NEW YORK:
D. APPLETON AND COMPANY.
1885.

WHY AND HOW.

 CHILDREN love pets; they never tire of stories; and they are delighted with jingle and the fun of incongruity. Mother Goose reigns supreme in the fairy-land of infancy. Through these loves the little opening minds may be led to careful observation, comparison, and descriptions—steps at once necessary to mental growth, and leading up to the portals of science. By insensible degrees, play may be made to merge in study, and fun take on the form of fact.

Upon these ideas of the basis and method of thought, this little work has been constructed. A few familiar nursery-rhymes serve to connect the present with the past thought of the child. The pet of the household — the cat — is studied. From the obvious in  structure and movement, the mind is led to see relations, and the adaptations of structure to functions and outward conditions. As each new animal is introduced, the study goes on by comparisons, showing resemblances and differences, and pointing toward scientific classifications.

This and kindred works will be of little use, however, if the lessons stop with the book. The whole intent of the method is to incite to a study of the animals themselves—the matter in the book directing attention, arousing interest, and serving as a guide to observation.

An endeavor has been made to present the pleasant side of animal life. To this end the affection, the intelligence, and the uses of our servants and friends have been dwelt upon, and ideas of violence have received but a passing notice. That we should be kind to animals is a necessary inference from observed relations, and this obviates the necessity of a formal exhortation or a cut-and-dried moral.

As a reader, this book is designed to supplement the regular reader of the grade. Common and familiar language is used, but no effort has been made to reduce the expressions to baby-talk, or to construct halting sentences with words of three or four letters only.

CONTENTS.

8 CONTENTS.—(*Continued.*)

Hey, diddle, diddle,
The cat and the fiddle,
The cow jumped over the moon;
The little dog laughed
To see the witch-craft,
And the dish ran away with the spoon.

OLD Mother Hubbard
Went to the cupboard,
   To get her poor dog a bone;
But when she got there,
The cupboard was bare,
   And so the poor dog had none.

WHAT THE CAT DOES.

1. COME, Jessie! put your kitty up in the cradle, and take a good look at her. She looks very pleasant. Can you tell us anything about her?

2. Yes! the other day I saw her come out of the barn with a mouse in her mouth.

3. She would lay the mouse down and let it run a little way, and then would pounce upon it and catch it again.

4. By-and-by she got tired of playing with it, and then she bit off its head and ate it up.

5. One day I saw her creep slyly along the ground and spring upon a little bird; but it flew away out of her reach.   In a little while I heard it sing up in a tree.

6. I was glad that she did not catch the bird, but she looked sorry.   When she catches birds, I think she is a naughty pussy; but perhaps she does not know any better.

7. I like to hear her purr, and have her rub against my hand, for then she is good and ready to play.   It is great fun to see her run round after her tail.

8. But sometimes she growls and looks cross, and then I am afraid to touch her for fear she will scratch me.

9. When she is hungry she comes and mews until she gets something to eat.   Some cats will jump upon the table and steal meat, but my kitty knows better.

10. She does not like dogs.   One day a strange dog came into the yard and barked at her.

11. Then her back came up, her fur stood out straight, and she growled and spit at him.

12. When he tried to bite her, she gave him a scratch on both sides of his nose, and ran up a tree out of his reach.

THE GRATEFUL CAT.

1. A LADY tells this pretty story of how a cat showed its thanks to a kind friend who had helped it in distress:

2. While living in a country place, one day the cat ate some rat-poison, but not enough to kill it. It was very ill, and cried like a little child. Its pain and heat were so great that it would dip its paws in water to cool them, though cats nearly always keep away from the water.

3. At last it went to the lady, and, mewing and looking up to her in a most pitiful way, seemed to ask for help. The lady took the poor thing in her arms, and tried in all ways she could think of to relieve it.

4. She bound it up in cool, wet cloths, and gave it medicine and gruel, and took care of it all day and night. The cat was soon better, and after a day or two it was as well as ever; and this was the way it took to show how thankful it was to the lady for her kindness:

5. One night, after she had gone up-stairs, she heard a mew at the window; and, upon opening it, there was the cat with a mouse in its mouth.

6. It had climbed up a tree that grew against the house, and, when the window opened, it came in and laid the mouse at the lady's feet. It rubbed against her, and purred loudly, as if it said, "See what a fine mouse I have brought you!"

7. The cat thought a mouse the best of all things, and this best it gave up for itself, and brought to its best friend, the lady.

8. This she did for a long time every day, and when, afterward, she caught mice for her kittens, one mouse was laid aside for the lady. If the kittens tried to eat this, she gave them a little pat, as if she said, "That is not for you."

9. After a while the lady would take the mouse, and thank puss with a pleased look and a kind tone, and then give it to the kittens, the cat looking on well pleased while they ate it.

WHAT THE CAT WEARS.

1. COME, Jes-
sie, take your cat in
your lap and look at her
again.   Can you tell something more about her ?

2. Yes ! Pussy has a thick coat of
soft fur to keep her warm, so that she
can run out of doors in cold weather.

3. She does not need to have clothes
like ours, and mamma does not ever have to mend
her coat.   Her fur all grows one way, and it is so
thick that, when it rains, the water runs off and
does not wet her skin unless it rains hard.

4. She likes to have me stroke her from her
head down, but she does not like to be rubbed the

other way. I know for one that it hurts more to have the hair pulled up than down.

5. She has long whiskers on each side of her mouth and nose, and some folks call them smell-ers. This is what I read about them in the "Cat's Picture-Book":

6. "I dare say you have seen a cat stick his whiskers out straight on each side of his face. Let us see what he does it for.

7. "Have you not seen a cat creep through a hole that seemed too small for him? I have, and I used to wonder why he did not stick fast.

8. "But Tom knows what he is about. He comes to the hole and spreads out his whiskers, and if they can get through without touching, he knows there is room for his body, and so he goes on."

9. Pussy's ears are large and stand up straight, so that she can hear the least nibble of a mouse, or the sly tread of a rat.

10. She has paws on her fore legs which she uses like hands. Her paws have each five toes, but her hind feet have only four toes each. Some few cats have more toes on each foot.

11. Dogs wag their tails when they are pleased, but pussy waves hers from side to side when the boys plague her, and she is angry.

"Who stole the
apples?"

"I," said dog Snow—"to play with, you know;
       I stole the apples."

"Who saw him steal?"
"I," said the cat—"mewed 'Snow, don't do that:
       Don't steal the apples.'"

2

PATCH AND THE MOUSE.

1. PATCH wa
cat that lived
house, and look
the rats and
came about. Sh
visit all
where
mouse-l
learne
doors
self

hold on to the handle of the door with one paw, and with the other raise the latch; then she would drop down and push the door open.

3. One evening, as the lady of the house was sitting at the fire before the candle was lit, Patch came into the room with a live mouse, and began to play with it.

4. The mouse watched his chance and ran into the bedroom, the door of which stood open. Patch followed, but could not catch him.

5. Pretty soon the cat came out of the bedroom in a great hurry. She went to the lady and mewed, and then went to the candle and back several times. The lady thought the cat acted queerly, and at last she got up and lit the candle.

6. Patch started off for the bedroom, and looked back and mewed, as if asking the lady to come also. The lady took the candle and went in to see what was the matter.

7. The cat at once went up to a curtain, put up her paw as far as she could reach, and touched it. The lady shook the curtain, and down dropped the mouse, which Patch caught at once. Mousey had run up the curtain out of reach, and so Patch went and got the lady to come and help her catch it.

1. Tommy was a famous mouser, and he kep
the house clear of rats and mice. He would catcl
birds, but he never ran after the chickens.

2. The hens were shy of him at first, but the
became used to him and would scratch just th
same while he was about. One day he was takin
a nap on the grass, and the chickens mounted upoi
his back and head, as you see in the picture.

3. This was too much for Tom; so he got uj
and went upon the porch to finish his nap, wher
the chickens would not disturb him.

HOW THE CAT MOVES.

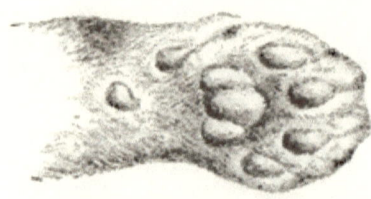

1. Now, Jessie, look at your kitty's feet and see if you can tell us how she can catch mice and birds so easily.

2. I will try. Pussy has long and sharp claws, but they are drawn back into her foot, so I cannot see them.

3. The bottoms of her feet are covered with a thick skin, so that it does not hurt her to walk over stones and rough places.

4. When I feel of her feet, I find that the bottoms are soft, so that kitty is able to move about without making a noise.

5. When she is hunting, she creeps along so quietly that the mouse does not hear her until she is so near that she can spring upon it.

6. Then her sharp nails come out, as you see in this picture, and the little mouse is caught by his coat and cannot get away.

7. I see that the nails upon her hind feet ar
not so sharp as those on the front ones. She doe
not catch mice with her hind feet, and so only th
nails of her fore feet need be very sharp.

8. When pussy runs up a tree, her sharp nail
hold on to the bark, and she uses her hind claw
as well as the fore ones. This is what I read in
book a little while ago about a cat's claws, and
thought it very strange:

9. "The claws of a cat grow very fast, jus
as our nails do, and, if the cat did not rub them ofl
they would grow so long that she could not us
them. So, when the cat feels that her nails ar
getting too long, she scratches something har(
until she wears them down to the right length.

10. "You have seen the cat stretching up anc
scratching the side of the door or a tree: this i
the way she has of paring her nails."

11. When pussy is angry or afraid, her shar
claws come out of her foot, and she makes read
to scratch.

12. My pussy knows that a dog is stronger ii
the jaws than she is; and so, when a strange do
comes about, she gives him a scratch with botl
her paws, and then gets into some safe place a
soon as she can.

DAISY AND HER PLAYS.

1. WHEN Nellie was a little girl, she had a present of a pretty white kitten, which she named Daisy, and the two soon became good friends.

2. While Nellie was at breakfast, the kitten would sit at her side, and once in a while it would reach up and touch Nellie's elbow, as if it said, "It is my turn now." When Nellie walked out, Daisy went along like a little dog, and at night she had a soft, warm bed by Nellie's side.

3. Little girls used to come and play with Nellie, and Daisy always took a part, and seemed to

enjoy the fun as much as the children did.   Or
of the games was hide-and-seek, and this Dais
soon learned to play as well as the best of them.

4. After this, at any time when Nellie woul
hide and call "coop," the kitten would jump u
and look about until it found her.

5. When Daisy grew up and had a kitten o
her own, she taught the young one the game sh
had learned.   The kitten would go and hide an
give one mew, and the old cat would search i
every corner of the room until she found it.

6. Sometimes the mother-cat would preten
not to see the kitten when close to its hidin[
place, and, when the kitten jumped out, Dais
would start back as though scared, just as childre
often do.

7. Then the two would roll over each othe
and race about and have a great romp together.

HOW THE CAT EATS.

1. This time, Jessie, I wish you would tell us something about the mouth of your cat, if you are not afraid she will bite you.

2. No! my kitty will not bite me; she knows I will not hurt her. Come, pussy, open your mouth and let me take a good look at it.

3. I see four long teeth in the front part of her mouth. The two on the upper jaw are the larger, but the two on the under jaw are the sharper.

4. When she shuts her jaws, these teeth would easily go through the skin and flesh of a rat or mouse, and very likely would break its bones.

5. Between these long teeth in front I can count six funny little teeth on each jaw. They

are too small to be of much use. Back of her lon
teeth I can see three or four on each jaw, an
these are sharp and stand up like saw-teeth.

6. When pussy licks my hand, I can feel the
her tongue is rough, and this is what I read abou
it in my cat-book:

7. "The cat's tongue is covered with littl
hooks, all pointing backward, so that when th
food is in her mouth, the rough tongue helps he
swallow it. With this rough tongue she laps u
milk, licks the plate clean when she is fed, an
licks the meat off from bones.

8. "The dog's jaws are strong, so he crushe
bones and eats the meat, bones and all; but th
cat's jaws are not strong enough for that, so sh
gets the meat off with her rough tongue."

9. My pussy keeps clean by licking her fur, th
hooks on her tongue brushing the dirt off. It
funny to see her wash her neck. She first lick
her paw and makes it wet, and then she reache
up to her neck and uses her paw like a brush.

10. The old mother-cat licks her kittens a
over, and keeps them clean before they can do
for themselves. She uses her jaws to carry he
kittens about before they can walk. She take
them up carefully by the nape of their necks.

OLD TOM AND THE EAGLE.

1. I WILL now tell you a story of a cat that made good use of his claws and teeth.

2. In a country place by the sea-shore an old eagle used to sail around in the air looking for something to eat.

3. If she saw a rabbit or a hare, or a little lamb or kid, she would pounce down and seize it in her strong claws, and fly away with it to her nest high up among the rocks.

4. The eagle became so bold at last that sh would swoop down and carry off a chicken fror the farm-yard close by the house.

5. One day old Tom, the house-cat, a big ol fellow, went out to take a walk, and, as the weathe was warm, he lay down in the sun to take a na near by where the rabbits lived.

6. This old cat had done a great deal of hun ing on his own account, and was not afraid of an\ thing he had ever met.

7. The eagle saw Tom as he lay there asleep and thinking she had found a nice, fat rabbit, sh pounced down upon him and carried him off.

8. Tom awoke and found himself sailin through the air at a great rate, while somethin pinched him very unpleasantly in the back.

9. He turned and struck his sharp claws an teeth into the eagle, tore out her feathers, and the tore into her skin and flesh.

10. The eagle thought she had found a quee rabbit, and tried to let him go ; but Tom held o and still tore and bit.

11. Soon the eagle began to lose strength an flapped slowly downward. At last she reache the ground so badly torn that she soon died, whil the cat ran off with only a few scratches.

HOW THE CAT SEES.

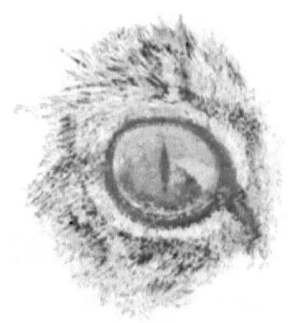

1. Now, Jessie, will you please tell us all that you have found out about your kitty's eyes?

2. Yes! When I looked at my pussy's eyes, in the bright sunshine, I saw that they are round and yellow, with a black streak in the middle running up and down.

3. The black spot in the middle of my eye is round, and I have read in a book that it is a hole to let in the light, and is called the "pupil."

4. The black streak in pussy's eye is the pupil, and it is almost shut up to keep out the bright light.

5. I looked into her eyes last night just before dark, and the pupil was large and round, as is shown in this picture.

6. When the pupil is opened so wide, more

light is let in, and pussy can see very well whe
it is so dark I can not see anything.

7. In this way, with her big eyes open, sh
sees and catches rats and mice that come out c
their holes in the night to get something to eat.

8. My kitty loves to sleep in the day-time o
the nice bed in her basket, or on the rug befoi
the fire. In summer she likes to go out and ge
a nap on the grass in the shade of a tree.

9. In the night, when she can see so well, sh
goes out to hunt and to make visits. When visi
ors come to see her in the night, we often hear a
awful squalling, which I suppose is a "cat's coi
cert."

10. In cold, winter nights, kitty mews to b
let in, and she then likes to curl up on my bed.

PUSSY'S VISIT.

"Pussy-cat, pussy-cat! where have you been?"
"I've been to London to see the Queen."
"Pussy-cat, pussy-cat! what saw you there?"
"I saw a little mouse under the chair."

MISS MUFFET AND FLUFFY.

1. Nobody knows where Miss Muffet came from. She walked into the kitchen one day and took her place by the warm fire, and she has been with us ever since.

2. Miss Muffet is a yellow-and-white cat. She is very quiet; but she likes fun for all that, and many a play the children have had with her.

3. When pussy had been with us about a year, we found her one bright May morning under the hedge in the garden with four tiny little kittens.

4. We got a basket and made a nice bed for them, and took them into the house. They grew

up to be playful kittens; but one day poor Tiny
kins fell into a tub of water and was drowned.

5. We liked
Fluffy the best; sh
looked so wise an
would do suc
queer things. W
found her one da
sitting in front c
a large open bool
and looking for all the world like a girl learnin
her lessons.

6. At other times she would sit all alone as i
she were thinking over some very serious matter.

7. One day we found them all
in the barn, where pussy had gone
to teach them to hunt mice.

8. We found that Miss Muffet
had caught a mouse, and put it
before the kitties, and Fluffy was
just ready to pounce upon it as
we came in. We gave a great

shout; two of the kittens sprang back to thei
mother, and one rushed head first into a large boo
that lay in one corner, and the mouse got away
Here is the story in verse:

FLUFFY AND THE MOUSE.

1. " Once there was a little Kittie
       Whiter than snow;
   In a barn she used to frolic,
       Long time ago.

2. " In the barn a little Mousie
       Ran to and fro;
   For she heard the Kittie coming,
       Long time ago.

3. " Two black eyes had little Kittie,
       Black as a sloe;
   And they spied the little Mousie,
       Long time ago.

4. " Four soft paws had little Kittie,
       Paws soft as dough;
   And they caught the little Mousie,
       Long time ago.

5. " Nine sharp teeth had little Kittie,
       All in a row;
   And they bit the little Mousie
       Long time ago.

6. " When the teeth bit little Mousie
       Mousie cried 'Oh!'
   But she got away from Kittie,
       Long time ago."

The Old House-dog.

HOW DOGS BEHAVE.

1. Now that Jessie has told us so much about her cat, we would like to hear about a dog. John, can you tell us something?

2. Yes! The dog in this picture is an old watch-dog. He is sitting by the chair, waiting for his master, and taking care that nothing is stolen from the room.

3. Our old dog Rover is always waiting for me when I get home from school, and the way he runs and jumps and barks, you would think he wanted to eat me up.

4. When I throw a stick he will run and bring it up, and if I try to get it he will hold on and growl, and pretend to be very angry; but he wags his tail and winks at me, to let me know that he is only in fun.

5. He is a good friend to our old Tabby and her kittens; but when a strange cat comes about, away he goes after her like the wind, barking with all his might. Then the cat goes up the nearest tree and spits at him.

6. When the children are at play, he follows them about to take care of them. He will lie down in the shade and go to sleep; but he keeps one eye open, and if anybody comes along, he is up at once to see if anything is the matter.

7. He loves to play with the children, and every day when nurse goes out with the baby, she gives him a ride on old Rover's back.

HOW NERO SAVED HIS MASTER.

Nero.

1. NERO was a dog that slept in a kennel in the yard to keep watch in the night, so that no thieves would come about and steal.

2. One night he followed his master up-stairs to his bedroom. The servant turned him out; but he howled and scratched at the door, and, when he was driven away, he soon came back.

3. At last his master, curious to see what he

would do, ordered the door to be opened. The dog at once rushed into the room, and, giving a little, short bark, by way of thanks, he crawled under the bed, as if he meant to stay there.

4. The master thought the dog acted rather strangely; but he soon forgot all about it, and, at the usual time, went to bed.

5. In the middle of the night a great noise in the room woke the master, and he got up to see what was the matter. There, on the floor, was a man flat on his back, while Nero stood over him growling in a way that said, " Lie still if you wish to keep a whole skin."

6. The man was tied and taken to prison, and he proved to be a robber who had come to steal the master's purse, and perhaps to kill him.

7. What made the dog leave his own bed and go up to the room of his master nobody knew; but he seemed to think that his master was in danger, and so he went up to help him.

8. You may be sure that Nero was well treated after this, and he could sleep where he pleased; but he went back to his kennel, as though he knew it was his place to keep watch out-of-doors.

9. He lived to be a very old dog, and he had the best of care until he died.

HOW DOGS LOOK.

1. WELL, John, we shall be glad to hear some-thing more about your dog to-day.

2. Here is a picture of Rover with a bird in his mouth. He has been trained to find the game that has been shot, and bring it to his master. When he takes the bird he is careful not to bite it.

3. Rover has a thick coat of long hair. It is not so fine as that of a cat, but it is enough to keep him warm in cold weather.

4. The cat has a round head, but Rover's head

is long and his nose is blunter than that of the
cat. Rover's ears are a great deal larger than
those of a cat, and they hang down by the side of
his head. Some dogs have ears that stand up and
point forward.

5. My sister has a little white terrier, Gyp,
whose hair is silky and much longer than Rover's,
and it hangs down over his eyes in a very funny
way. He can see very well for all that.

6. Dogs do not hunt for rats and mice; but if
a rat comes in sight when Gyp is about, he gives
one bound and a snap, and there is a dead rat.
When Gyp is asleep, if we call out "rats," he
springs up and rushes about as if he were crazy.

7. When the cat is angry she lashes her tail
from side to side, but when the dog is angry he
holds his tail out straight and stiff.

8. When the dog is glad he wags his tail as
though he would wag it off. When the little
black-and-tan dogs are very glad, you can't tell
whether the dog or the tail wags most.

9. The cat does not like to go into the water,
but Rover likes nothing better than to swim out
after a stick which I have thrown in. In summer
he goes into the water every day to keep himself
cool and clean.

WHAT MUNGO DID.

1. Once on a time a miller had a large shaggy dog called " Mungo." He slept at the mill nights, and took care that no thieves came about.

2. He was very fond of the children, and, when baby pulled his hair with both her hands, he looked pleased and would not let anybody know how much she hurt him.

3. In the morning, Mungo would place himself on guard at the upper doorway, while the miller went to look after his work in the lower part of the mill.

4. As soon as the miller came up, Mungo, without being told, would start for the house to get

his master's breakfast. He made two journeys, bringing a pitcher of milk and a dish of oatmeal tied up in a napkin.

5. One morning there was a flood in the river, and a little dog living near by fell into the stream and was carried down yelping with all his might.

6. Mungo was coming with his master's breakfast, as usual, when he heard the cry of the little dog. He set the dish down by the side of the path, and dashed off down stream as hard as he could run.

7. When he had got well below the little dog, he sprang into the river, and swam out into the middle of the stream, just in time to catch the helpless dog as he was swept down.

8. Mungo seized him by the neck in such a way as to keep his head above water, swam with him safely to the shore, and dragged him high and dry out of the water.

9. After shaking himself, he cuffed the little dog first with one paw and then with the other, as much as to say, "Now, you little dunce, keep away from the river."

10. He then went back to where he had left the dish, and carried it to his master as usual.

HOW DOGS USE THEIR FEET.

1. To-day, John, we should like to hear some-thing about the dog's feet and how he uses them. Have you something to tell us?

2. Yes! One way the dog gets about is by swimming. Last summer little Harry fell into the river when no one was near by, and Rover swam in and brought him out.

3. The folks made a great fuss over him then; but he did not mind it, only he seemed glad that Harry was not hurt.

4. I find my dog has just as many toes as a cat.

His nails are longer than those of the cat, but not so sharp. They are big and strong, but he can not draw them back into his foot.

5. He can not climb a tree, as his nails are not sharp enough, but he can dig a big hole in the ground when he is after a rabbit or a squirrel.

6. The bottoms of his feet are harder than those of a cat, and he can run all day in rough places without hurting them.

7. With his hard feet and long nails he makes more noise when walking than a cat; but then it is no matter, for he does not have to catch mice and rats.

8. Rover can not open a door, but he raises his paw and raps or scratches until somebody comes and opens it for him.

9. Ask him to shake hands, and he will hold out his paw as well as anybody can, though he has not learned which is his right and which is his left paw.

10. When Gyp is hungry, it is funny to see him. He will whine a little, and then sit up straight and hold out his paws like a little beggar.

11. Then, if you offer him something to eat, he sniffs at it, and, if he does not like it, turns up his nose and goes off. He likes candy as well as I do.

1. A DOG with a fine bone in his mouth set out to cross a stream on a narrow bridge.

2. As he was crossing, he looked into the water and thought he saw another dog with a bone much finer than his own.

3. Being a very greedy dog, he dropped his own bone and made a snatch at the one he saw; and so, by trying to rob another, he got a good ducking and lost his dinner.

1. In a great city a man had a place near the river, where he blacked boots and shoes.

2. To get more custom, he had a little dog who would roll himself in the mud, and would then rub against the feet of people as they passed by.

3. After a time the trick was found out, and the man and his dog were sent away where they could make a more honest living.

1. To-day we would like to find out about a dog's mouth and teeth. John, have you something to tell us?

2. Yes! When playing with Rover, last night, he opened his mouth, and I had a good chance to see what was inside.

3. His teeth are like those of the cat, only larger and stronger, and his jaws are so strong that tramps run away when he offers to bite them.

4. When Lion, the old bull-dog, gets his grip on anything, the only way to make him let go is to open his jaws with a bar of iron.

5. The cat uses both its claws and teeth in catching game; but the dog can bite so much harder, that he does not need sharp claws to help him.

6. When a dog eats, he swallows large pieces of meat without chewing, and he will crush a bone

to get all the meat and the marrow inside.   After
he has eaten off the meat, he often swallows the
bone.

7. His tongue is not so rough as that of a cat,
but he laps water and milk with it, and he loves
to lick the hands and faces of his friends.

8. In summer, when it is very warm, the dog
does not sweat as we do, but he opens his mouth
and pants, and the water runs off from his tongue.

9. When the dog is well, his nose always feels
cool; but if he is ill, his nose gets warm.

10. It is funny to see how old Rover will act
when some one comes around whose looks he does
not like.

11. He just stands up straight and his hair
begins to rise.   Then he raises his upper lip so as
to show his long teeth, and gives a very low growl.

12. Next he steps forward a little and gives
two or three short and snappish growls, and then
somebody would better look out.

13. One day my mother was coming up the
lane, and met a tramp, who made a motion to take
hold of her.   Rover made one spring, and his jaws
snapped.   The fellow yelled, and, as he ran away,
he limped as though he had been hurt.   Since
then he has not been about.

LUPO AND TINY.

1. "Lupo" was a very large dog with a thick, white coat. He was so good-natured and faithful, that his master felt that the children were safe when Lupo was about.

2. In winter Lupo liked to stretch himself before the fire, and, when he did so, he took up the whole hearth-rug, and there was no chance for any one else.

3. "Tiny," the little terrier, liked the fire as well as Lupo, but could find no place where it was not either too cold or too warm.

4

4. So she would climb up on to Lupo, and use him as a bed. It was very funny to see her tread round and round, as dogs do when they make up their bed, and then nestle down into his long hair and go to sleep.

5. When Tiny had her bed all right, she would not let Lupo move. If he stirred, she would fly at his head and bark and growl in a most spiteful way.

6. Then, if he did not stop at once, she would bite his long ears, and Lupo would sink back and lie as quiet as a lamb.

7. When out following the carriage, Lupo did not seem to notice little dogs, and, when a half dozen at once set upon him, he just shook them off and kept on his way.

8. But he was not always so good-natured. When a big dog came in his way, he seemed to feel that it was a duty to whip him.

9. There would be a growl and a snap, and away would go the other dog over Lupo's head, with a piece of his hide gone or some of his bones broken.

10. As Lupo could not be broken of this habit, whenever he went out his master would put a muzzle on him so he could not bite.

HOW DOGS SEE AND SMELL.

1. I think John has something new to tell us about his dog to-day.   Let us listen to him.

2. I have looked at my dog's eyes, and I find that the pupil is round, like mine, and it does not shut up into a streak, as in a cat.

3. The dog does not see so well in the night as a cat, but his sense of smell is much more keen.

4. My uncle has a pointer-dog named "Grouse," and one day I went out with them to hunt quails.

5. Grouse would run all about until he smelled the birds, and then he would creep along a little way and stand still with his nose pointing forward.

6. My uncle would then come up with his gun, and, when he was ready, the dog would go slowly forward scaring the birds up, when uncle would shoot them.

7. In this picture we see a dog pointing quails among the reeds. The birds hear him, and are just ready to fly.

8. A dog will follow the track of his master for a long distance, and hounds will follow the track

of a wolf or a fox or a bear, so that the hunter can come up with it and kill it.

9. Rover is a good watch-dog, and, if he hears or smells anybody about in the night, he makes a great racket.

10. He knows, too, where the other animals belong, and, if a cow or a pig gets into the garden or yard, he goes and drives it out.

PUFF AND THE BABY.

1. PUFF was a tiny little terrier and a great pet. He came by his name from a way he had of making a great fuss, and getting out of breath about nothing. Baby was crazy to get hold of him, and, when she saw Puff, she would wriggle out of any one's arms to get to him.

2. The children needed only say, "Baby, Puff is coming," when she would give a crow of delight, and out went her little arms, fingers, and legs, all working together.

3. But Puff's hair was long and his skin tender, and, when baby's fingers got hold of him, his howls were dreadful, and he never got away without leaving some of his coat in baby's fingers.

4. One day baby was asleep on the sofa, and Puff thought it was a good time to look at her, now that he could do so without fear. It was funny to see him creep along, peering into the little sleeping face, but ready to start back in a moment.

5. He went closer and closer, until his little cold nose touched baby's mouth, when she woke with a sudden start, threw out her two little fat hands, and seized him by the whiskers.

6. Puff pulled and howled and backed off the sofa, dragging the baby after him; but she fell on top of him, and was not hurt.

PUFF AND THE RAT.

1. WHEN Puff would lie quite still out of doors, with his nose pointed one way for a long time, the children knew what was the matter.

2. There was a rat somewhere about, and Puff had seen him go into his hole and was watching for him to come out.

3. The boys would get a spade and begin to dig, and, when they had got in a little ways, Puff would take the matter into his own hand, and dash into the hole.

4. His little, short paws would make quick work, and he would dig in until even the tip of his tail could not be seen.

5. Then a squeak would be heard, and Puff would back out with a rat in his mouth, which he knew what to do with to prevent being bitten himself.

6. He would fling the rat into the air, and, as it would come down, he would catch it by the nape of its neck, give it a shake or two, and it was dead.

7. How proud he was then! He would lay the rat down in different places to see where it would look best, and then he would carry it round to each one in the house, until somebody took him and scrubbed the dirt off, so he was fit to be seen.

1. HERE we have the picture of a boy and a pony. The boy is taking a ride; but he has stopped, and seems to be waiting for some one.

2. Now we must find out something about the horse, and, Charlie, I think you can tell us what we wish to know.

3. I can tell something how a horse looks and what he can do, for we have horses at home, and I help take care of them.

4. The horse is much larger than the cat or dog. His home is in the stable, and he does not come into the house, as they do.

5. His head is long, and, when he puts his nose to the ground, the top of his head is just about as high as the top of a flour-barrel.

6. His eyes are large and round; his nose is much wider than that of a dog, but he has smaller ears than some dogs, and they stand up straight.

7. Upon the top of his head, and along the top of his neck, he has a thick bunch of long hair, which is his mane.

8. He has a broad, strong back, and can carry a man all day without being very tired. There is

room upon his back for two persons, and sometimes two ride at a time.

9. He has long legs, so that his head is about
as high as the top of a man's hat.

10. He is covered with a thick coat of short
hair, and this keeps him warm, except in very cold
weather, when he needs a blanket.

11. Instead of claws, he has hoofs, hard like
bone, so that it does not hurt him when he trots
or runs on the ground.

12. When horses work, or travel over a hard
road, they have iron shoes nailed to their hoofs, so
that they will not be hurt by striking the stones.

13. The hoofs have no feeling on the outside,
and it does not hurt the horse
to have these shoes nailed on.
They grow like our nails, and
must be pared once in a while.

14. The horse can paw
with his fore feet, and kick
with his hind ones, and, when
he kicks hard, he breaks
things. He has a tail covered
with long hair, and this he
uses as a switch to keep off
flies in summer.

Full Speed.

THE HORSE AND ITS FRIENDS.

1. In some places men keep   horses
to ride when they go out to hunt   foxes, and
these horses are called hunters.

2. Dogs are also used in the hunt, and the
horses and dogs are so much together that they
often become the best of friends.

3. Once old "Hector," a dog, had such a liking
for his friend "Ben," the hunter, that he would
leave his own bed and go and sleep with Ben in
the stable.

4. In the morning when Hector was let out, Ben would be very uneasy until he came back, and, when he came, the horse would give a joyful neigh.

5. Ben would stoop his head, and Hector would lick it all over, and then Ben would scratch Hector's back with his teeth.

6. One day when they were out together a big dog set upon Hector and threw him down, and began to bite and tear him.

7. Ben saw the danger his friend was in, and rushed forward to help him. The strange dog felt a grip in the back, and then he was thrown so far that he was glad to be able to get up and limp away. He never tried to touch Hector again when Ben was about.

8. Here is another story of a horse and his friends: A poor stray kitten found its way into a stable and made its home there.

9. It soon made friends with a lame chicken and the pony, and the three were never quite happy except when together.

10. It was very funny to see the kitten and the chicken close together upon the pony's broad back, while he would stand very still so as not to disturb them.

HOW THE HORSE EATS.

1. To-day we wish to find out something about a horse's mouth, and how he eats. Can you tell us, Charlie?

2. Yes! I have looked at the horse's mouth, and can tell about his teeth. In front, on each jaw, he has six teeth with sharp edges. These cut the grass when he feeds in the pasture.

3. Next back of these are four sharp teeth, one on each side of each jaw, and these are sometimes called tusks. They are in the same place in the jaw as the long teeth of the dog, and with them the horse can tear things.

4. Next back of the large teeth there is a place where there are no teeth, and this is the place 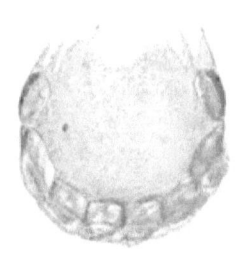 where the bit of the bridle goes when we ride the horse or drive him in a carriage.

5. Next back are six broad, flat teeth, on each side of each jaw, and with these the horse grinds his food before he swallows it.

6. In summer, if our horses have not much to do, we turn them out to pasture, where they eat grass. In winter we give them plenty of hay and oats, and, when they work, we always feed them with grain.

7. Horses will eat grain of any kind, but they seem to like oats best. We sometimes feed them with corn-meal instead of oats.

8. The teeth of a horse change in looks every year until he is eight or nine years old, and men who are used to horses can tell how old they are by just looking at their teeth.

9. The horse does not lap his drink like a cat and dog, but he puts his mouth into the water and swallows whole mouthfuls. He will sometimes drink two or more large buckets of water at a time.

1. "BILLY" was a fine pony, brought from Shetland for a little boy to ride to and from school, as the distance was too great to walk. When Billy first came he was barefoot, and when he began his daily-journeys he was shod for the first time.

2. The blacksmith who put on the shoes lived quite a long distance from Billy's home, and the pony had never been over the road but on the day he went to be shod. A few weeks after, the

blacksmith saw Billy, without halter or bridle, coming up the road toward the shop.

3. Thinking the pony had strayed away, the blacksmith turned him round, and threw stones at him to make him go back toward home.

4. The pony trotted off; but the blacksmith had only fairly got to work again, when he heard a noise, and, looking up, there stood Billy at the door.

5. This time, before driving him away, the blacksmith took a look at his feet, and found that Billy had lost a shoe. He at once made a new one, and put it on, and then waited to see what Billy would do.

6. The pony looked at the blacksmith for a moment, as if asking whether he was done; then he pawed, to see if the new shoe was all right, gave a neigh for a "thank you, sir," and set off for home on a brisk trot. His master knew nothing about the matter until next day.

1. To-day we are to find out what the horse is good for. Charlie will tell us whether the horse is of any use on the farm.

2. We could not get on very well without horses on the farm. They are very strong, and will do a great deal of work that a man can not do.

3. They carry us on their backs, and draw great loads that half a dozen men could not move.

4. With them we plow and harrow and prepare the ground for planting. If we did not have horses, or other animals that can do the same kind of work, a man could only plant a little patch that he could dig up with a spade.

5. They draw loads of grain and fruit to mar-

ket, and bring back what is needed on the farm. They draw in the hay in summer and bring up the wood in winter. They take to market the things which we raise on the farm, and bring back the goods which we buy at the store.

6. They will work from morning till night, in all kinds of weather, and are ready to get up and be off whenever they are needed.

7. When they have a heavy load, they walk along slowly; when a light one, they trot along quite rapidly. But if the doctor is needed, some-body jumps on the back of a horse, and off he gallops like the wind.

8. Then we harness the horses to a light wagon and take a ride; sometimes we go on a visit, some-times to mill, sometimes on a picnic, and on Sun-days we go to church.

9. In the winter, when snow is on the ground, horses draw sleighs instead of wagons. The sleigh makes but little noise in slipping over the snow, and a string of bells is put upon the horse to let people know that the sleigh is coming, so that no one need be run over.

10. When we go out sleigh-riding, all wrapped up in blankets and robes, the horses scud along, the bells jingle, and we have a gay time.

The Stage-Coach.

1. HORSES, when they do not work too hard, love to play and have fun. They will race after each other, kick up their heels, and have a merry time. Here are two stories which a man tells of the kind of fun that the horse seems to enjoy :

2. "One of our horses, 'Billy,' used to give us a great deal of trouble, he knew so much. He had found out how to untie his halter, and open the stable-door, and so would get out when the

door was not locked. One day Billy came out, and found little Harry in the yard. He did not attempt to hurt the child, but drove him into a corner, and kept him there by shaking his head whenever the little fellow tried to get away.

3. "I heard Harry cry, and led Billy away; but he gave a parting shake of his head to the boy, as much as to say, 'Next time I will look after you closer.'

4. "Coming home one evening, I heard a couple of horses running and frisking about in the farmyard at a great rate. The wall was high, and I could only see their heads, and once in a while a whisk of their tails.

5. "I found a hole to look through, and saw that the horses were amusing themselves by chasing a pig around the yard.

6. "They would drive it into a corner, and fling their heels into the air with great delight. They would not give the poor pig a moment's rest.

7. "They would rest for a few minutes, and the pig would settle down to his cabbage-leaf, when they would rush at him from different sides, so that he had not the least idea where to run to get away from them."

1. WE see, from what Charlie has told us, how useful the horse is. We now would like to have him tell us how we should take care of horses.

2. I will do so by telling a story. Last Saturday Uncle William hitched old Major and Ben to a big wagon, and took a load of boys to Oak Hill, to pick berries and have a good time.

3. I tell you uncle knows what boys and horses want, if anybody does. Pretty soon Bobby Jones wanted to drive. So uncle gave him the reins.

4. Bobby wanted the whip, too; but uncle

said that we should not whip the horses, as they went fast enough. He carried the whip just to touch them up when there was any danger.

5. Then Bobby began to jerk the reins; but uncle showed him how the horses would move one way or the other by pulling the rein a little, and he told Bobby that jerking hurt their mouths.

6. When we went down Stony Hill, just before we came to the long bridge, uncle took the reins, and drove slowly, because, he said, it would make the horses lame to drive fast down hill.

7. As we were crossing the bridge, uncle jumped out to see what was the matter with old Major, who was limping a little, and he found one of his shoes was loose. Uncle pulled the shoe off, and threw it into the wagon, and then walked the horses until we came to the blacksmith's shop, on the other side of the bridge.

8. Then they took old Major into the shop, and the blacksmith pared the hoof and set the shoe. In nailing on the shoe, he said he must be careful not to drive the nails too far in where the hoof was tender, or it would make the horse lame.

9. In going up Oak Hill, uncle would stop the horses every little way to let them rest. They would pant for a minute or two, then take a deep

breath and go on. There was a cool spring close by, where we stopped to go into the berry-field, and here we hitched the horses in the shade.

10. They were very warm and thirsty, but uncle would not give them any water until they had time to cool. The flies were awful, but our horses switched them off with their long tails.

11. Near by was a little bob-tailed horse turned out to pasture; and, as he could not switch off the flies, they bit him so he could hardly get time to eat. If the man who owned that horse could have the flies bite him so for a few days, I don't think he would cut off the tail of another horse.

12. We just filled our baskets with berries, and ate our dinner under the shade of some big trees that stood by the spring. Then we came home.

13. Uncle's horses are steady, because he uses them well. He never jerks them, or whips them, or yells at them. When he goes near them they rub their noses against him, they are so glad to see him.

14. In winter he puts blankets on them when they stand still, for he says their coats are not thick enough to keep them warm. Then he gives them a good bed of dry, clean straw to lie on, and plenty of hay and grain to eat.

A ride, and what came of it.

Good Morning.

1. On the other page we see a boy on the back of a donkey, taking a ride. The donkey looks kind and steady, but look below and see what has happened!

2. We will call upon Harry to tell us something about the donkey—how he looks, and what he can do.

3. The donkey is much like a horse, only smaller. His head is larger and more clumsy than that of the horse, and his ears are much larger.

4. His nose is blunter than that of a horse, and his legs are shorter. He has some long hair between his ears, but no mane on his neck. His tail is long and slim, with long hair only on the end of it.

5. His feet have hoofs like those of a horse, but they are smaller, and he can travel in many places where a horse can not.

6. His coat is longer and thicker than that of

the horse, and he can get along with much less care. He goes along with his head hanging down, as if it was too heavy for him to hold up, and he looks very awkward beside the horse.

7. He has teeth like those of a horse, so that we can put a bit in his mouth when we drive him.

8. In color, most donkeys are brown, or a dirty white, with a black stripe along the back, from the head to the tail, and also a black stripe across the shoulders.

9. When the horse neighs, his voice is very pleasant; but the donkey's bray is loud and harsh, and when he opens his mouth his voice is heard above all others.

10. I read the story of a man riding a donkey in the West, when the Indians caught him. As they were about to carry him off, the donkey gave an awful loud bray, which scared the Indians, so that they ran away and left the man to go on his journey.

1. Poor, old donkey! In some countries he is made to do all kinds of hard and dirty work, and he is driven about with many blows and kicks.

2. The rag-man, in the city, picks up a load for him out of the gutters; and the tinker, who

goes about mending old pans and kettles, loads him down with heavy tools.

3. There are people that have no homes, but rove about and drive donkeys in queer little carts, and camp by the way-side, and sleep out-of-doors.

4. For them a donkey is better than a horse, for he can live upon coarse food. He eats thistles and weeds that a horse will not touch; and he will pick up enough to eat where a horse would starve.

5. In places by the sea-side, or among the mountains, where people go to stay in hot weather, donkeys are kept for ladies and children to ride.

6. In the morning, long rows of them will stand waiting for ladies to come and hire them. They are so kind and steady, that there is no danger to the little children who ride them.

7. The donkey is very sure-footed, and will carry his rider safely over steep and stony places where a horse can not go. Poor, old donkey! He looks stupid, and he is slow. But, when treated kindly, he is a very willing and faithful servant.

1. THE donkey is not as stupid as he looks, and he has often shown that he knows what he is about, and that he is able to take care of himself.

2. In the picture we see a little girl with a donkey going to market, and as Dick is always treated kindly, he is ready to do all he can for her.

3. A man who bought a donkey for his children, tells this story of him: "I did not allow him to be pounded, and he got something better to eat

than thistles. My donkey proved to be no fool; but, like others, who have more wit than good manners, he was forever getting into mischief, and leading others into it.

4. " He could open all the gates, and climb all the fences; and many a morning he woke me by braying in the midst of my field of wheat. I was obliged to sell him, as he knew too much about doors and gates, and was too cunning to be kept."

5. A man once set his bull-dog to attack a donkey that was grazing near the river. For a while the donkey kept his heels toward the dog in such a way that the dog could not get at him.

6. Watching his chance, the donkey turned and seized the dog by the nape of his neck, so that he could not use his jaws, then dragged him to the river, plunged him in, and lay down upon him, keeping his head under water until he was drowned.

FIDDLE-DE-DEE,
The cat was at tea,
The rabbit
was taking
snuff,
The dog and the pig
Were dancing a jig,
And the donkey
put on a lace
ruff.

Oxen at Work.

HOW THE COW LOOKS.

1. Among our four-footed friends the cow comes next, and we wish to find out something about her. Will, do you think you can help us?

2. Yes! Since we began these lessons I have watched our cows, and have found out some things that I did not know before.

3. The cow has a heavier body and shorter legs than a horse. She has a short neck, and a long tail, with a bunch of coarse hair on the end

6

of it.   Her head is larger than that of a horse, and
her nose is wider.   Her ears stand out on each
side of her head, and above them she has a pair of
horns that spread out.

4. Her hoof is not round, like that of a horse,
but is split into two parts, and is called a cloven
hoof.   She has a thick coat of coarse hair, which
keeps her warm in all but the very coldest
weather.

5. In front, the cow has six teeth on her under
jaw, but none on her upper jaw.   In place of teeth
is a ridge hard as a bone.   In the back part of her
mouth she has six broad, flat teeth on each side
of each jaw, with which she chews her food.

6. Cows are of different colors.   Some are
red, some are black, some are white, and some are
spotted or striped.   I have seen one kind that
looked like a black cow with a white blanket on.

7. When the cow eats grass, she swallows it
without chewing.   When she has enough, she
stands still or lies down, and the grass comes up
into her mouth in little balls, and these she chews
fine and swallows again.

8. The ball she chews is called a "cud," and
she will chew one cud after another, until she has
chewed up all the grass she has eaten.

1. THE OX is very strong, and can do work like a horse. When oxen are used, two are put together with a wooden yoke on their necks.

2. Oxen can draw large loads, and can work a long time without being tired ; but they are so slow that they are not used much, except on farms.

3. In summer, cattle run in the pasture and live upon grass. They gnaw it off close to the ground, and they feed most of the day.

4. In the middle of the day, when the weather

is hot, they lie down in the shade, or stand up to their knees in the water, to keep cool.

5. At night the cows are driven to the farm-yard and milked, and in the morning they are milked again and driven back to the pasture.

6. In winter, cattle are kept in the stable, or in the farm-yard where there is a shed that they can go into when it storms or is very cold.

7. They are fed with hay ; but cows that give milk, and working-oxen, are fed with grain also. Beets and turnips are sometimes fed to cattle.

8. When cattle stand in the shade chewing their cud, there is no other animal that looks so mild, and pleasant, and happy.

9. The cow is very fond of her calf, and licks it over several times a day. If anybody hurts the calf, he must look out for the old cow's horns.

10. I have heard of a little lamb that had lost its mother, and was put into a lot with six cows. After a time he was taken out and put with the other sheep. But they all fought him, and he was sent back to his old pasture.

11. The cows all rushed up to meet him, and he ran to each in turn. Then one cow licked him all over, and he was passed to the next, and so on until all had done the same thing.

1. CATTLE do not hunt rats and mice like the cat, nor watch like the dog, nor do we ride them as we do a horse or a donkey; but in some ways they are more useful to us than any of the others.

2. When Johnny sat down to breakfast this morning, a cow gave him that bowl of fresh, rich milk, which he ate with his bread. Then, when we drank the nice cup of coffee that mamma had made, the cow gave us the cream which we put into it.

3. When the dinner was put up for school, the cow gave the cheese and the butter that was spread upon the bread. In the nursery rhyme "Little Miss Muffet sat on a tuffet, eating the curds and whey" which the old cow gave her.

4. This morning Johnny's hair was in a snarl, and mamma got it out with the help of the old cow, who gave the horn to make the comb.

5. When we go out in wet weather, the cow gives her hide to be made into the leather out of which our coarse boots are made; and the calf gives its hide for our fine boots and shoes.

6. When our new room was plastered, a little while ago, the cow gave the hair to mix with the mortar, so that the plaster would stick together and stay on the wall.

7. Before we get our chairs and tables, the cow takes off her hoofs and gives us the glue with which they are put together. Then Santa Claus could not bring Johnny his white-handled knife till the old cow had given a bone for the handle.

8. "Sleepy-head goes to bed" at night, and the candle he carries is another present from the old cow. The flesh of grown cattle that we eat we call beef, and the flesh of calves, veal.

1. WE will now take a look at our friend, the sheep. See it stand there, looking so kind, and harmless, and innocent!

2. The sheep is much smaller than a cow, and in size is like a large dog. Its nose is more pointed, and its ears are smaller, than those of a cow. It has small, cloven hoofs, and it eats grass and chews its cud in the same way that a cow does.

3. Its jaws are like those of a cow, with no teeth in its upper jaw in front, and with broad, flat chewing teeth back. Like a cow, it feeds upon

grass in the summer, and upon hay and grain in the winter.

4. The rams have large horns that twist about in a very curious way. Lambs are playful, like kittens, and they hop and frisk about, and they sometimes have great games with old Rover or with the cat.

5. Sheep are covered with a thick coat of wool, and this keeps them warm, so that they can live out-of-doors in the coldest weather. In summer their "fleece" of wool is sheared off. The

Head of Merino Ram.

wool is made into cloth, and the cloth is made up into clothes for folks to wear, so that the coat of a sheep makes the coat for a boy.

6. Besides our clothes and blankets, the sheep gives us fine, thin leather to bind books and make gloves, and tallow to make candles and soap. The flesh of sheep, which we eat, is called mutton.

1. SHEEP appear very helpless, but when they run wild they know how to take care of themselves very well.

2. They butt with their heads, and the large, old rams will run very fast, and strike a fearful blow.

3. When a flock of wild sheep is feeding, one is placed at some distance out on each side, to keep watch.

4. If an enemy is seen, the guards give a kind of whistle, and the whole flock scuds away to the rocks on the mountain.

5. If they can not get away, they place the lambs in the center of the flock, and the old sheep face outward, the biggest rams in advance.

6. When the fox or the dog are within a few yards, the rams rush at him, and they are nearly always successful in killing or driving him away.

7. The ewe has so strong a love for her lamb, that she will face any danger to protect it.

8. One day a shepherd saw a fox in a high, rocky place, trying to get a young lamb; but the old ewe kept her head toward the fox, and gave him no chance.

9. At last the fox made a spring and seized the lamb, and at the same time the ewe struck him with her head, and they all went over the rocks and were killed.

10. A kind of sheep in South Africa have tails so large and fat, that the people tie them to small carts so that the sheep can get about. The fat is used for butter.

1. In many ways the goat is like the sheep. It is about the same size, and has the same kind of teeth and hoofs, and it eats the same kind of food. It has a thick coat of hair. Some goats have fine hair that is made into cloth and nice shawls.

2. All the goats have spreading, sharp horns, and the billy-goat has a long beard, which hangs down almost to the ground. The kids are playful, like lambs, but they are shy, and do not like to come near folks.

3. The goat is more active than the sheep; it can run faster and jump higher, and it climbs rocks where a sheep can not go.

4. The billy-goat is apt to be cross, and then he runs and butts anything he meets.

5. Like the cow, the goat gives us milk, and butter, and cheese. It also gives fine leather for ladies' shoes and for binding books, and the kid gives us soft leather which is made into gloves.

6. Goats do not live in large flocks like sheep, but they go about three or four together, and will pick up a living where a sheep would starve.

7. They are so sure-footed that they will climb up the sides of steep rocks, wherever they can find a place to put their little pointed hoofs.

1. THE hog is about as large as a sheep, but its legs are shorter.   It has a cloven hoof, but it does not chew a cud like the sheep.

2. It has a long, blunt nose called a snout, and this it can move about to smell something to eat. It can use its snout, also, to root up the ground for seeds and other food.

3. Its ears are large and lop over; and it has a queer little curly tail.   It has four large pointed teeth, called tusks, and with these it can inflict worse wounds than a dog.

4. It is covered with coarse hair called bristles. Brushes of nearly all kinds are made of the bristles. The hog is kept warm not by its hair, but by its fat, which lies just under its skin.

5. Swine eat almost all kinds of food, and they eat a great deal and very often. When feeding at a trough, they root each other out of the way, and seem in a great hurry to get all they can.

6. When a pig is caught, or is hungry, it sets up a fearful squeal, which is worse to bear than the bray of a donkey.

7. When the pig runs out in a pasture, it roots up the ground so much that a ring is put through the thick edge of its snout ; then, when he tries to root, the ring hurts so he stops.

8. It is not best to meddle with little pigs, and make them squeal, when the old sow is about, for she is ready to fight for them at any time.

9. The flesh of swine is called pork, and when salted and smoked it is bacon.

THERE was a little piggie wig,
 So fat it couldn't run :
With eyes that twinkled merrily,
 And tail that curled with fun.

This piggie had a little trough,
 Which was always filled with food,
Bran and broth, and turnips too,
 And everything that's good.

Its little bed was made at night
 Of lovely meadow hay ;
There, covered up all but the nose.
 It snored till break of day.

With sleeping and with eating,
  The piggie grew so fat,
That at last it couldn't walk or run.
  So on the straw it sat.

At length it grew so *very* fat
  It really couldn't see;
But the fatter, still the jollier,
  And so it laughed "He! he!"

At last, one day, a strange man came;
  Alas for piggie then!
For all at once it went away,
  And was never seen again.